Bear cave
for sale
P.O. Box 9214071

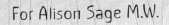
Bear Sports Day
SUNDAY 10AM

BEAR
BOOGIE
Saturday
7PM

For Alison Sage M.W.

First published in 2013 by Hodder Children's Books

Text copyright © Martin Waddell 2013
Illustrations copyright © Lee Wildish 2013

Hodder Children's Books, 338 Euston Road, London, NW1 3BH
Hodder Children's Books Australia, Level 17/207 Kent Street,
Sydney, NSW 2000

A catalogue record of this book is available from the British Library.

ISBN 978 1 444 90678 3

Printed in China

Hodder Children's Books is a division of Hachette Children's Books,
an Hachette UK Company

www.hachette.co.uk

HELP
NEEDED!
Bear Wood
Gardening Day

BEAR
FESTIVAL
Friday
1PM

BEAR WOOD
PICNIC
Sunday 12PM

WANTED
HONEYPOTS
P.O. BOX 93416180

BEAR WOOD

Bears, Bears, Bears!

Martin Waddell and Lee Wildish

h

Hodder Children's Books

A division of Hachette Children's Books

Ruby liked bears so
she put up a sign.

BEARS
WANTED
FOR
PLAYING
with RUBY xx

BEAR WOOD →

Along came a bear.
"I'm a bear from Bear Wood,"
said the bear. "Will I do?"

"You're just what I wanted," said Ruby.
Ruby and the bear played games:

bear hug...

bear chase...

and bear hide-and-seek.

"More bears!"
cried Ruby.

"Am I not enough?"
asked Ruby's bear.

94, 95, 96, 97

"More bears mean more fun!" cried Ruby. So Ruby's bear sent out to Bear Wood for more bears.

Two little bears came from Bear Wood and they played with Ruby.

"More! More!" cried Ruby. So Ruby's bear sent out to Bear Wood again and a bunch of party-loving, ring-a-ding bears turned up.

One cool bear played the piano
and sang, and some of them
danced on the patio.

They all wanted to dance with
Ruby, and they whirled and
twirled until she was puffed.

But she still cried,
"More! More! More!"
And more and more bears
came from Bear Wood.

Some of them took
Ruby paddling down
at the creek.

The moon rose over Bear Wood
as Ruby came sleepily home.

Back at her house, the bear party was still going on. There were bears in the cupboards and bears on the stairs. Bears looking at pictures and climbing on chairs. There were bears everywhere!

Five bears were snoring in Ruby's bed.
"I'll sleep in the bath!"
Ruby said, grabbing a
blanket off the bears.

But there was a bear
in the bath playing
with boats. Two
bears were queuing
to get in the shower.
Three bears were
looking for towels. And
the littlest of all the bears
was curled up in the basin.

"THERE ARE TOO
MANY BEARS!"

cried Ruby.

"I thought there might be," said Ruby's bear. And he yelled: "BEARS OUT!"

Straight away the bears hurtled out of Ruby's house.

Bears **climbed** through the windows.

Bears **squeezed** up the chimney.

Bears **shot** through the doors.

Bears **popped** out from under the floors.

Everywhere there were bears,
running off into Bear Wood!

"Now you've only
one bear left,"
said Ruby's bear.

"One bear
is just what
I wanted,"
said Ruby.

BEAR
GRILLS
BQ
TIPS

Honey

Made
with
LOVE
RUBY xxx